LITTLE RACCOON
AND NO TROUBLE AT ALL

BY LILIAN MOORE · PICTURES BY GIOIA FIAMMENGHI

LITTLE RACCOON

AND NO TROUBLE AT ALL

McGRAW-HILL BOOK COMPANY

New York   St. Louis   San Francisco   Düsseldorf   Johannesburg
Kuala Lumpur   London   Mexico   Montreal   New Delhi   Panama
Rio de Janeiro   Singapore   Sydney   Toronto

Also by Lilian Moore

TONY THE PONY
BEAR TROUBLE
LITTLE RACCOON AND THE OUTSIDE WORLD
LITTLE RACCOON AND THE THING IN THE POOL

For HELENE FRYE

"Little Raccoon," said his mother, "Will you help?"

Little Raccoon jumped up.
"Do you want me to go to the running stream?"

"No," said his mother.

"Do you want me to get some crayfish
for supper?"

"No," said his mother. "I want you to listen.
Mother Chipmunk and I must go to the
outside world. Will you take care of
her two baby chipmunks till we get back?"

"Will you, Little Raccoon?"
asked Mother Chipmunk.

Little Raccoon looked at the baby chipmunks.
"I never did *that* before," he said.

The two chipmunks sat very still,
looking up at Little Raccoon.

"See how good they are,"
said Mother Chipmunk.
"They will be no trouble at all."

So little.
So good.
And no trouble at all.

"All right," said Little Raccoon.
"I will take care of them."

"Thank you, Little Raccoon,"
said Mother Chipmunk.
Mother Raccoon thanked him, too.
And they went away.

Little Raccoon stood looking
at the baby chipmunks.

"He's my brother," said one.
"She's my sister," said the other.

"Oh," said Little Raccoon.

The chipmunks sat looking
at Little Raccoon.
"Play with us," said the brother.
"Play follow me," said the sister.

"I never did *that* before,"
said Little Raccoon.

"All you do is follow us,"
said the brother.

The chipmunks ran to a tree.
"Come on!" they cried.
"Follow us!"
And they ran up the tree.

Little Raccoon ran up the tree, too.

One chipmunk ran out on a branch.
Whoosh!
He jumped into the next tree.
"Follow me!" he cried.

The other chipmunk
ran out on the branch, too.
Whoosh!
She jumped into the next tree.
"Follow me!" she cried.

Little Raccoon ran out on the branch, too.
But the branch was too small for him.
Crash!
He came tumbling down.

"Follow us!"
cried the chipmunks.
And they ran to the old stone wall.
There was a hole in the wall,
and one chipmunk ran inside.
The other called, "Follow me!"
And he ran into the hole, too.

Little Raccoon picked himself up
and went over to the wall.
"This game is hard work,"
he thought.

"Come in! Follow us!"
called the chipmunks.

Little Raccoon stuck his head into the hole.
Then he put his front paws in.
But the hole was too small for him.
"I can't get in," he said.
He pushed with his back paws.
"I can't get out!" he cried.

18

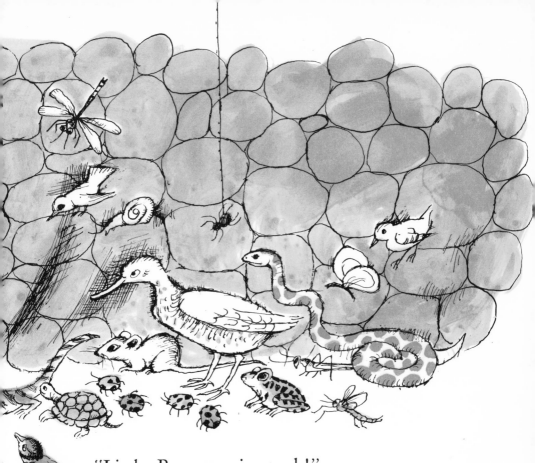

"Little Raccoon is stuck!"
said the brother chipmunk.
"You look funny!" said the sister.
And they began to laugh.

Little Raccoon did not think it was funny.
He began to wiggle. This way and that.
And he pushed and pushed.

At last with a wiggle and a push,
he came tumbling out.

The chipmunks ran out of the hole.
"Here we are!" they cried.

"No more games!" said Little Raccoon.
"You sit here and you sit there."

The little chipmunks sat very still,
looking up at Little Raccoon.

"Do you know any tricks?"
asked the brother.

"No," said Little Raccoon.

"We know a good one," said the sister.
"Can we show you?"

"What's the trick?"
asked Little Raccoon.

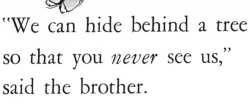

"We can hide behind a tree
so that you *never* see us,"
said the brother.
"Never!" said the sister.

"But all I have to do
is go around the tree," said Little Raccoon.

"Try it," said the brother.

And the chipmunks hid
behind a tree.

Little Raccoon went around the tree,
but the chipmunks went
faster. He did not see them.
"Are you there?" he asked.

"Yes!" cried the chipmunks.

Little Raccoon went
around the tree again.
Around and around.
To his surprise, he still
did not see the chipmunks.
He went faster and faster.
Around and around.

All at once the world was going
around and around, faster and faster.
Little Raccoon was so dizzy he had to sit down.

"Here we are!" cried the chipmunks.

"No more tricks," said Little Raccoon.
"You sit here and you sit there!"

The little chipmunks sat very still,
looking up at Little Raccoon.
"I'm hungry," said the sister.
"So am I," said the brother.

"And so am I!" thought Little Raccoon.

He looked at the baby chipmunks.
"Do you like crayfish?" he asked.

"We like butternuts and beechnuts,"
said the brother.
"And hazelnuts and hickory nuts,"
said the sister. "What's crayfish?"

"It's the best of all!" said Little Raccoon.
"Let's go to the running stream and get some."

The chipmunks jumped up.

"Stay right behind me!"
said Little Raccoon.
And off they went.

On the way Little Raccoon
thought about crayfish.
Ah! Crayfish!
He began to sing:
  "Ah! Crayfish! Crayfish!
  It's an eat-it-every-day fish."
And he sang it again and again.

Soon he saw Old Porcupine,
resting by a tree.

"Hello, Little Raccoon," said Old Porcupine.
"Where are you going all by yourself?"

"All by myself?" said Little Raccoon.
And he turned around to look. "Oh no!"

"What is it?" asked Old Porcupine.

"I've lost some chipmunks," said Little Raccoon.

Just then something hit Little Raccoon
on the head.

"Here I am," the brother chipmunk
called from a tree.

Something hit Little Raccoon
on the head again.

"Here I am!"
called the sister chipmunk.

"Come down!" said Little Raccoon.
"Come right down!"

The baby chipmunks came running down
from the tree.
"Here we are!" they cried.

Little Raccoon looked at them.
"I must do something,"
he thought.
"I must do something
to make them behave."
But all he said was, "Follow me."
And they went on
to the running stream.

Up the stream was the beaver pond.
And there was Beaver,
working on his house
in the middle of the pond.

Little Raccoon looked at Beaver.
"I must do something," he thought,
"and I know what it is!"

Little Raccoon began to fish.
The chipmunks sat and looked at him.
They saw him catch
a fine, fat crayfish.

They saw him jump into the water
and swim out to Beaver's house.

Little Raccoon sat there
and ate the crayfish.
"Oh," he called to the chipmunks,
"This crayfish is *so* good!"

"We want some!" said the chipmunks.
"We want some!"

"Beaver," said Little Raccoon,
"The chipmunks want to come out here.
"Will you give them a ride?"

"Hop on!"
said Beaver to the chipmunks.
And he took them to Little Raccoon.

"You sit here," said Little Raccoon,
"and you sit there."
And he gave them some crayfish.

Then Little Raccoon jumped into the water
and swam back across the pond.

He began to fish again,
and soon he had a fine, fat crayfish.

The little chipmunks
looked across the pond
at Little Raccoon.

"We don't like crayfish," said the brother.
"We *hate* crayfish," said the sister.

Little Raccoon went on eating.

"We don't like it here," said the brother.
"We don't like it at *all*."

Little Raccoon went on eating.

"We want to go home!" said the brother.
"Little Raccoon," cried the sister,
"We want to go home."

Little Raccoon looked
across the pond
at the chipmunks.

"No more games?" he said.

"No," said the chipmunks.

"No more tricks?"

"No," said the chipmunks.

"No more tree fun?"

"Oh no!" said the chipmunks.

"Beaver," said Little Raccoon,
"The chipmunks want to come back."

"Hop on!"
said Beaver to the chipmunks.
And he took them back across the pond.

"Stay right behind me,"
said Little Raccoon.
"All the way home!"

That's what the chipmunks did.

And all the way home,
Little Raccoon sang:
      "Ah! Crayfish! Crayfish!
      It's an eat-it-every-day fish."

They got home just as
Mother Raccoon and Mother Chipmunk did.

"Hello, my little ones,"
said Mother Chipmunk.
"Were you good?
Were they good, Little Raccoon?"

The chipmunks looked
at Little Raccoon.

Little Raccoon looked
at the chipmunks.

"No trouble at all,"
said Little Raccoon.